The Mouse Who Ate the Moon

Petr Horáček

WALKER BOOKS
AND SUBSIDIARIES

LONDON · BOSTON · SYDNEY · AUCKLAND

One evening Little Mouse
peered out of her hole.
She was looking at
the moon.

"The moon is beautiful,"
she thought, as she settled down to sleep.
"I would love to have a piece all of my own."

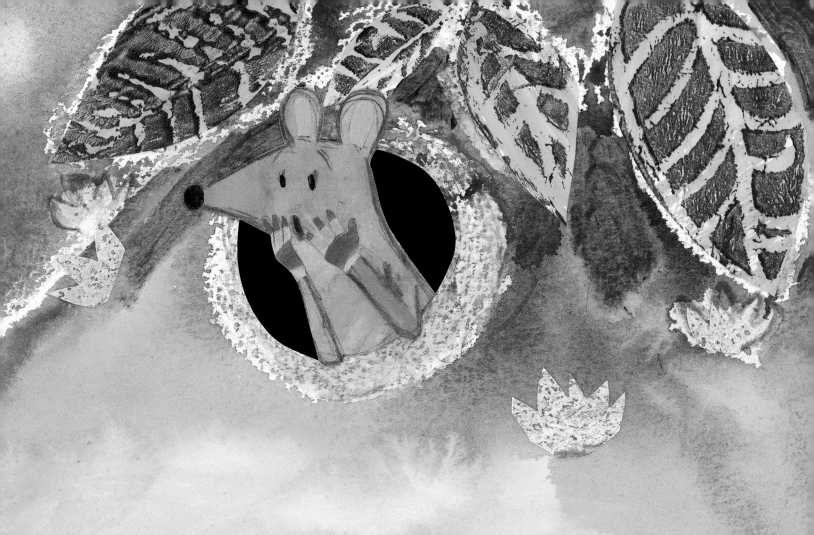

Next morning when Little Mouse
woke up, she saw something that
she had never seen before.
A piece of the moon had
fallen from the sky.
"My wish has come true,"
she cried.

Little Mouse ran to get
a closer look at her piece of
moon. It smelled delicious.

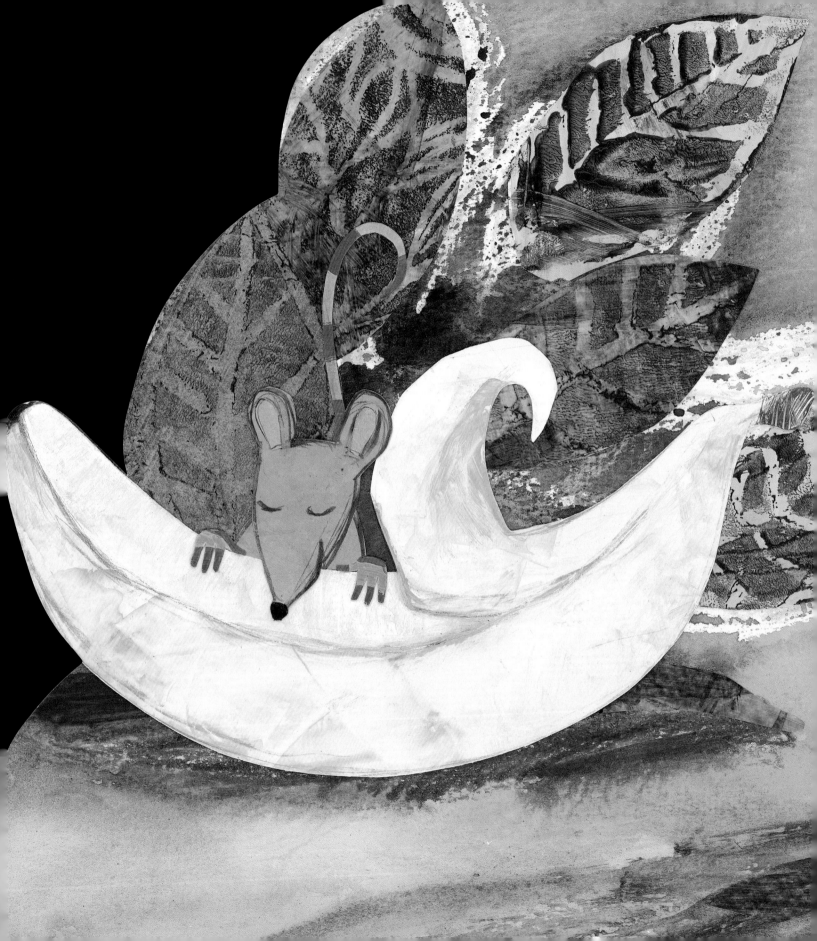

"Perhaps I can eat it,"
thought Little Mouse.
"It smells so good. I'll just
have a tiny nibble."

So she took a tiny bite,
and another,
and another,
and just a tiny bit more,
until ...

she had eaten half of it.
"Oh no!" thought Little Mouse.
"Now the moon won't be
round any more."

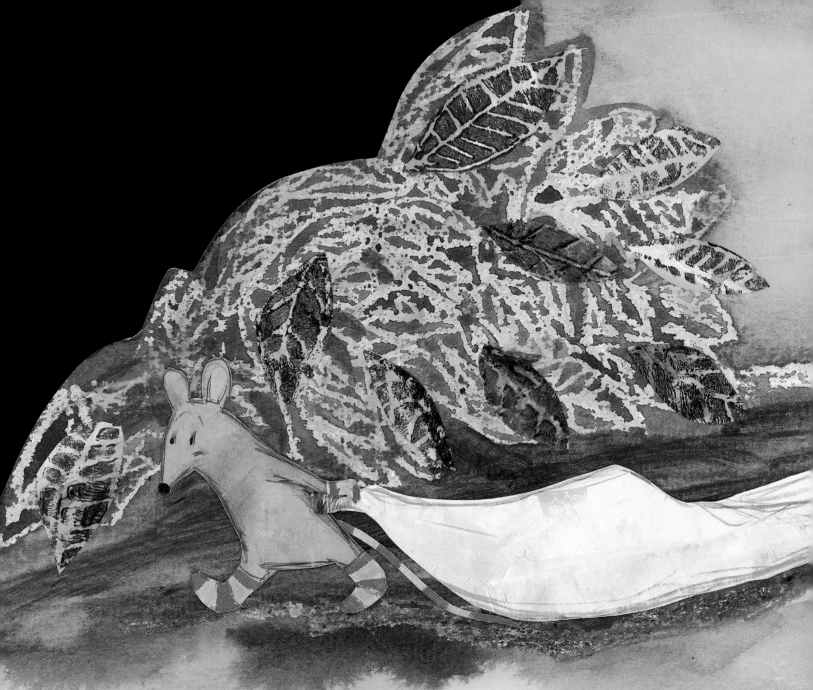

"What's the matter, Little Mouse?" asked Rabbit.
"I have eaten some of the moon," said Little Mouse,
"and now it won't be round any more."
"Nobody can eat the moon," said Rabbit.
"Well, I just did," said Little Mouse.

She walked past Mole's house.
"What's the matter, Little Mouse?" asked Mole.
"I have eaten some of the moon," said Little Mouse,
"and now it won't be round any more."

"Nobody can eat the moon,"
laughed Mole.
"Well, I just did,"
said Little Mouse.

Little Mouse sat in her hole, sadly
looking at the remains of the moon.
It began to get dark.
Then she heard Rabbit and Mole.
"Little Mouse, come out," they said.
"We want to show you something."

Little Mouse followed Rabbit
and Mole to the top of the hill.
They sat and looked at the starry sky.
Slowly something shiny appeared
behind the trees.

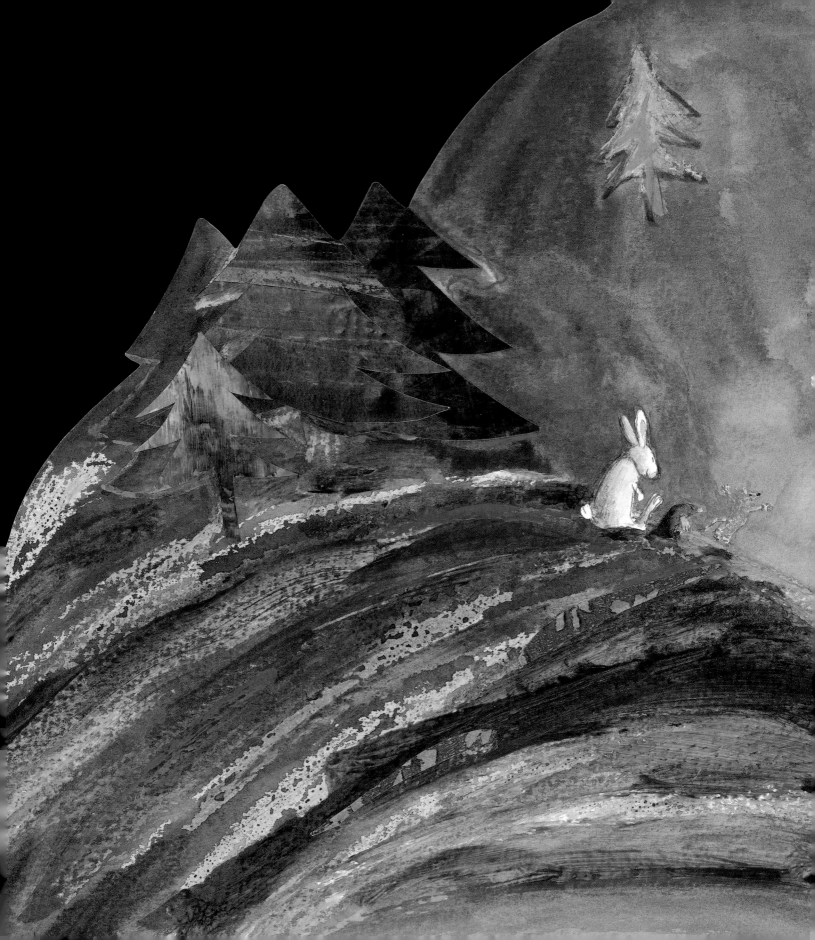

It was the moon.
It was big and it was round.
Little Mouse was overjoyed.
"Look at the moon!" she cried.
"I haven't eaten it after all."

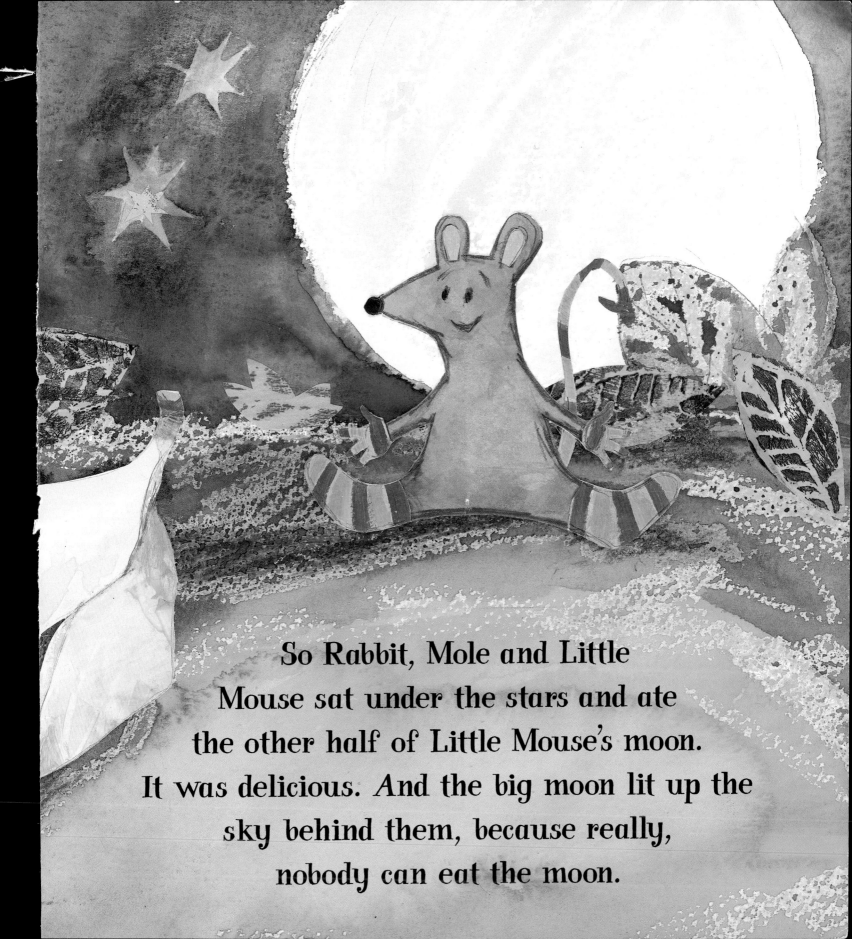

So Rabbit, Mole and Little
Mouse sat under the stars and ate
the other half of Little Mouse's moon.
It was delicious. And the big moon lit up the
sky behind them, because really,
nobody can eat the moon.